GW00374851

"Unless someone like you cares
a whole awful lot, nothing is
going to get better. It's not."

Dr. Seuss, The Lorax

With special thanks to:

Linda Birkin
Chris Calveley
Zoë Channon
David Smith

First published in 2022 in Great Britain by
Wildlife Whimsies Publishing
www.wildlifewhimsiespublishing.co.uk

ISBN 978-1-9996246-5-1

Characters and text copyright © Tina Talbot 2022

Illustrations copyright © Judit Matthews 2022

The right of Tina Talbot and Judit Matthews to be identified as
the author and illustrator of this work has been asserted by
them in accordance with the Copyright, Designs and Patents
Act of 1988.

All rights reserved. No part of this publication may be
reproduced, stored in a retrieval system, or transmitted in any
form or by any means, electronic, mechanical, photocopying,
recording or otherwise, without the prior written permission of
the publisher.

A CIP catalogue record for this book
is available from the British Library.

Printed in Great Britain

The
Powerful Pollinators

Day and Night

Tina Talbot

Illustrated by Judit Matthews

WILDLIFE WHIMSIES PUBLISHING

CONTENTS

1. THE BEES

Betty was abruptly awoken from her daydream by a burst of laughter. "You were daydreaming again, Betty," her fellow worker bees giggled. Betty, who was young and impulsive, did not like anyone laughing at her.

"Stop laughing at me!" she lashed out. "Or I will challenge you to a sword fight with my stinger!" Betty turned round and boldly lunged her bottom at them. The other worker bees looked at each other and laughed again.

"We are not laughing at you, Betty. We love that your dream is to become one of the Queen's special guards, the Stingerteers, but don't forget that you are younger than us, so your stinger hasn't quite developed yet. You can't defeat us in a duel nor protect the Queen."

"I can beat you in a duel!" Betty insisted, thrusting her stinger at the worker bees.

"Betty, you must learn to calm down. Think before you act, or you will get into trouble," Molly, one of the worker bees, advised her. Betty put her little stinger away and murmured under her breath. "I will become one of the Queen's Stingerteers. They'll see!"

"Betty! Stop grumbling and get back to work! We are all terrified of the Queen, and you know what will happen if we displease her; she will banish us from the colony," Molly scolded. "It's bad enough that she makes us do all the jobs inside and outside the hive just because we're girls; she doesn't even use our names; she calls us her worker bees, and we're not allowed to take a break. It's not fair! The boy bees don't do anything except keep her company. She calls them her drones; I wish I were a drone," Molly sighed.

"No, you wouldn't," replied another worker bee. "When the Queen finishes with a drone's company, he dies! I think our lives are better than theirs. Anyway, we have wasted far too much time chatting; we must prepare for the ball this afternoon. Remember what the Queen said, nothing is to go wrong; if it does, we will all be punished."

"Wait!" cried Betty. "Why is the Queen throwing a ball?"

"She wants all the bees in the land to put their differences aside and become friends so we can all help each other against our common enemy, the bee-killing wasps," another worker bee answered. "She has invited all the honey bees, bumblebees and solitary bees to the ball, including her guest of honour, Princess Mina, the Tawny mining bee."

"Why is Princess Mina so important?" asked Betty.

"She helps the oil beetles survive," answered Molly as she signalled everyone to get back to work. "Oil beetles are pollinators," she explained.

Betty was not scared of the

Queen like the other worker bees; instead, she was overcome by a flood of admiration for her and, with even more determination to prove that she was worthy of her attention, she returned to her chores with renewed vigour. "I WON'T let the Queen down, and I WILL become one of her special guards!" she told herself.

That afternoon, a steady flow of black and golden-coloured bees arrived at the entrance of the beehive, which was now heavily protected by the Queen's regular guards. The guards, ordered to be on high alert for potential imposters, took it in turn to patrol the garden. They flew to the ivy-covered house where a family and their pet cat lived. Then, over a little wooden shed, past a small oval-shaped pond, which looked more like a battle zone between butterflies and dragonflies than a peaceful oasis, and back to the hive in the vegetable patch by a white picket fence at the bottom of the garden.

The guards were on the lookout for any predatory wasps that might be trying to sneak into the hive, in particular, their mortal enemies, the killer yellowjacket and beewolf wasps. "You must be vigilant," the Queen told her guards.

One by one, the guests entered the ballroom, including Princess Mina, whose beautiful ginger-coloured fur made her stand out from the crowd. They buzzed with excitement, thrilled at the prospect of meeting Her Majesty the Queen. The worker bees worked tirelessly to make the guests happy, ensuring they had plenty of pollen and nectar to eat and mopping up any subsequent nectar spillages from the floor.

The Queen went round the ballroom and spoke to all her guests individually, giving them her full attention. She made them feel welcome and told them how important it was for all of them to work as a team. She looked round to find Princess Mina, but she could not see her, so she left the ballroom and searched the hexagonal honeycomb cells just in case she had decided to make a tour of the beehive. However, when it became evident that Princess Mina had gone missing, the Queen started to worry. Not wanting to arouse suspicion, she discreetly flew to her chambers and summoned Polly and Amber, her two special guards, the Stingerteers.

"At your service, ma'am," they said as they bowed to their Queen.

"I have a crucial job for you both, which you must carry out with the utmost discretion," the Queen instructed. "Princess Mina has disappeared. She is my responsibility; if the bees find out she has gone missing, they will turn against me. You must find her. Do not fail!"

"You can rely on us, ma'am; we will not let you down." Polly and Amber bowed and immediately took leave of her.

In the ballroom, Betty was busy serving the guests. She looked up momentarily and noticed that the Queen's Stingerteers were amongst them. "That's strange," she thought. "Something must be wrong!"

Betty put down the tray of nectar she was carrying and watched Polly and Amber closely. "They are looking for something," she perceived. "I must follow them! I need to cause a diversion, so I can leave without being seen." Betty took some nectar from the tray she had put down and deliberately spilled it on the floor, knowing that the housekeeper worker bees would go into a frenzy.

"EMERGENCY SPILLAGE! ALL HANDS ON DECK!" screamed one of the housekeepers. In the panic and commotion that followed, Betty snuck out unnoticed and followed the Stingerteers.

"She's not in any of the rooms," Betty overheard one of the Stingerteers say. "Let's look outside the beehive just in case she has gone into the garden." Betty quickly hid in one of the cells as Polly and Amber flew past.

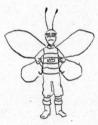

"I wonder who's missing?" Betty thought. She quietly flew back to the ballroom, hid behind one of the guests and surveyed the room. The honey bees and bumblebees were all there. She counted the solitary bees, and realised that there was one missing, then she caught her breath when she worked out who it was.

"Oh no! Where's Princess Mina?" Panic-stricken, she accidentally bumped into the guest she was hiding behind and knocked her nectar over. "I'm sorry," she apologised, mopping it up from the floor. She looked up at the guest and noticed that she was wearing a yellow jacket. "That's strange," Betty thought, but in her urgency to find Princess Mina, she didn't give it a second thought.

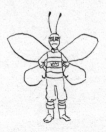

Betty looked everywhere. She searched the upper part of the comb where the honey was stored and then checked the cells in the rows below that kept the pollen. She peeked into the nursery in the lower section, where the babies were looked after and almost bumped into a worker bee rushing to fetch royal jelly for the Queen to eat. Nevertheless, Betty could not find Princess Mina anywhere. She passed through the passageways along the honeycomb edges when suddenly she heard something unusual. "What's that noise?" Betty asked herself. She took a closer look and, there, wriggling and trying to free her wings from the rope that bound them, was Princess Mina. Betty immediately flew over and began to untie her.

"YOU, THERE! STOP!" Betty froze in fear. She slowly turned round and came face to face with the Stingerteers.

"It's not what you think," pleaded Betty. "I noticed that Princess Mina had gone missing, so I decided to look for her."

"Stand aside, worker bee. You are not one of the Queen's Stingerteers. Move away from the Princess," Amber instructed.

"I want to help you. I want to be one of the Queen's special guards,"

Betty implored. Polly and Amber looked at each other and laughed. "You are too young to be one of the Queen's special guards; your stinger has not developed yet. Now, leave us alone to do our job," ordered Polly.

"No!" Betty insisted.

"Then, we will fight you with our stingers!" Amber threatened.

Betty impulsively stood her ground. "Come on then, fight me with your stingers. I am not scared." Polly and Amber looked at each other and laughed again.

"You are funny, worker bee. Now, I'll ask you for the very last time, stand aside," Amber ordered.

Ignoring them, Betty continued to untie the Princess. Amber's patience was running thin; not wanting to hurt

Betty with her stinger, she pushed her away. Betty rolled over, hit her head on the passage wall and fell unconscious to the floor.

The Stingerteers flew over to the Princess. However, before they could finish untying her, they felt a blow to their heads and they fell to the ground in a daze. When they eventually came round, they found themselves tied up as well. Meanwhile, Betty woke up and realised that the Stingerteers were in trouble; she immediately flew over to them but had to turn back when she heard voices approaching. She quickly hid on the floor where she had hit her head.

Polly and Amber discreetly looked up and saw two wasps with menacing yellow and black markings. "Our plan is working," Beewolf told Yellowjacket.

"We knew that if we kidnapped Princess Mina, the Stingerteers would go looking for her, leaving the Queen unguarded. Now, we can kill the Queen and take over the hive. Just think of all that honey that will be ours! Let us signal the wasps waiting outside to ambush the hive and kill all the bees in the ballroom. The wasps will rule the kingdom!" Beewolf declared.

However, the wasps did not know that Betty was there, listening to every word they were saying. Remembering what Molly had told her, she decided not to be hasty but to stay calm instead. "I must warn the Queen!" she thought sensibly. Betty quietly flew past the wasps and raced to the Queen. "Your Majesty, you are in grave danger! You must summon all your guards now! Polly, Amber and

Princess Mina are tied up and have been taken hostage by Beewolf and Yellowjacket. They want to kill you, ambush the bees in the ballroom, and take over the kingdom!"

The Queen immediately took charge. "I will alert my guards. Thank you, worker bee. Now, go back and help Polly and Amber," she ordered. "My guards will be with you imminently." Betty flew back as quickly as she could and jumped on Beewolf, but the wasp was too powerful for Betty; she pushed the little bee away, got her stinger out and flew towards her. Amber and Polly managed to untie themselves and race to Betty's rescue just in time to save her. At that moment, Yellowjacket flew over to help

Beewolf.

"On guard!" Polly warned the wasps. "We are the Stingerteers, the finest sword fighters in the land, and we will defend our Queen to the death!" The bees lunged at the wasps, their stingers met, and they engaged in a fierce battle of wills; both sides determined to win. After a relentless fight, the wasps weakened first, and the bees defeated them. While they were fighting, Betty had taken the opportunity to untie Princess Mina and set her free.

The Queen entered the room with her guards, who captured the wasps and locked them in one of the cells. The Queen then ordered Polly and Amber to help the other guards defend the hive from a swarm of wasps that had amassed outside. "Worker bee, you stay here with Princess Mina and me," the Queen commanded Betty.

"Yes, ma'am!" Betty replied.

It was a difficult battle, but the guards managed to fend off the wasps with the help of the Stingerteers. Polly and Amber immediately flew back to the Queen and told her the good news. "Let's go back to the ball and pretend nothing has happened," the Queen ordered, with a sigh of relief, knowing that she and the Princess were now safe. "We must make a pact to never speak of this incident." Polly, Amber, Betty and Princess Mina solemnly promised the Queen they would not tell anyone.

They returned to the ball, where everyone was unaware of what had just happened. The Queen introduced the Princess to all her guests, Betty resumed her duties, and the Stingerteers joined the regular guards at the entrance, just in case any rebellious wasps decided to return. The ball was a huge success, and the Queen triumphed in uniting all the bees in the land.

When all the guests had left, the Queen summoned Polly, Amber and Betty to her chambers. "I have asked you here because I want to express my gratitude to you all for saving Princess Mina's life," she said. "Worker bee, I especially want to thank you for warning me just in time; your actions have saved the lives of many bees, and you have shown me that you are reliable and responsible. What is your name?" she asked Betty.

"Betty, ma'am."

"Betty, you are too young to protect me at present, but I will move you from working inside the hive to working outside as one of my pollinating bees, and as soon as your stinger has grown, you will join the Stingerteers and become one of my special guards. You may now go." The Queen waved her wing to indicate that she wanted them to leave.

Polly and Amber flew over to Betty. "Thank you for helping us, Betty. We could not have saved Princess Mina without you. When you join us, we will be The Three Stingerteers!" Betty was ecstatic. She returned to her fellow worker bees with a huge smile on her face.

"Why are you so cheerful?" asked Molly, "and where have you been?" Betty looked at them with love and affection.

"Nowhere. Just busy working, that's all," Betty replied with a gleam in her eye.

As she helped her friends clean the ballroom before starting her new duties as a pollinator, she noticed a piece of folded paper stuck in some nectar that had dripped onto the floor. She picked it up and unfolded it. There was a mysterious message inside:

TO BETTY

YOUR PRESENCE HAS BEEN
REQUESTED

GO TO THE VEGETABLE
PATCH AT SUNRISE

2. THE BUTTERFLIES

"ATTENTION!" yelled the New Recruits Squad Leader. "Look at you! You are the sloppiest bunch of recruits I have ever had the misfortune to lay my eyes on!"

The New Recruits Squad Leader, whose code name was White Admiral, looked at the row of newly emerged butterflies in front of him and wondered how he would ever turn them into secret agent ecosystem indicators.

The butterflies had been hand-picked to attend the most prestigious spy school in the land. Hidden in a secret location in a large, empty field, the nearest signs of civilisation were a vegetable patch and a white picket fence that belonged to an ivy-covered house about half a mile away.

White Admiral folded his black and white wings, looked at the six recruits and made a quick assessment of them. He was very pleased to see a Grayling butterfly in the group. His neutral brown wings were the ultimate camouflage, making him the perfect undercover agent on top secret missions in places where he could blend into natural backgrounds like soil, stone and tree bark. His code name was Grayling.

The other recruits, code-named: Adonis Blue, Red Admiral, Painted Lady, Clouded Yellow and Green Hairstreak, were a beautiful array of blue, black and red, orange, yellow and green butterflies. Their bright colours made them ideal masters of disguise, able to impersonate natural objects like flowers and leaves and also scare their enemies into thinking they were poisonous.

    "LOOK AT ME WHEN I'M TALKING TO YOU!" yelled White Admiral, bringing his thoughts back to the task at hand. "I am splitting you into two teams. Agents Grayling, Painted Lady and Green Hairstreak will be in Team A, and Agents Adonis Blue, Red Admiral and Clouded Yellow, will be in Team B," he continued. "At the end of your training, there will be two missions awaiting you to accept; one is more dangerous than the other. I will choose the best of you to lead the most dangerous one. Now, get out of my sight and report back for your physical training tomorrow at 0600 hours sharp!" shouted White Admiral.

The two teams immediately went indoors to their dormitory, where they would spend the next few nights sleeping and began unpacking their belongings. Adonis Blue, menacingly, looked over at Grayling as he emptied the contents of his backpack. "Let's make things difficult for Grayling," he said to his teammates. "After all, he does not belong here with us; his neutral colours make him common. We are all special because we have bright coloured wings." Clouded Yellow and Red Admiral agreed to go along with his plan.

Meanwhile, Grayling looked over at the two butterflies in his team. He was nervous because he wanted to make friends with them, but he didn't know if they wanted to be friends with him. He plucked up the courage and made his move, smiling and introducing himself to his teammates. "Hello," he said. "I'm Grayling." The two butterflies instantly smiled back at him.

"Hello Grayling. My secret agent name is Painted Lady, but you can call me Lady," said the orange butterfly.

"My secret agent name is Green Hairstreak, but just call me Hairstreak," said the green one.

The three of them happily chatted for a while before going to bed. Grayling put a picture frame with a photo of his baby brother, a little caterpillar, on his bedside table and contentedly drifted off to sleep.

The following morning, the alarm

woke the butterflies up at 0530 hours.

As Grayling got out of bed, he noticed that his picture frame had fallen off the bedside table. He then heard the butterflies in Team B laughing and realised they had deliberately knocked it off. Deciding to ignore them, he picked up the photo frame and placed it back on the bedside table. "Don't take any notice of them," Lady and Hairstreak told him, reading his thoughts. Grayling smiled at his new friends, and the three of them walked out and prepared to face the stern White Admiral.

"Well, at least you miserable lot have made it here on time," White Admiral continued in his formidable way. "In the next two days, I will teach you combat training, how to go unnoticed amongst the wildlife and most importantly, how to spot a crisis in the ecosystem. You are the .eyes and ears of nature. If you notice anything wrong in the environment, you MUST report it to me IMMEDIATELY. Do you understand?" he asked the recruits.

The six butterflies replied, "Yes Sir, White Admiral Sir!"

White Admiral was not impressed. "I can't hear you!" he bellowed.

YES! SIR! WHITE ADMIRAL SIR!" they shouted back.

"Good. Now I want you to get into your teams," White Admiral instructed as he turned round to pick up some skipping ropes. Grayling, Lady and Hairstreak took the opportunity to have a quick chat. "I think we're going to have trouble with Team B," Lady said.

"Yes, I don't think they like you, Grayling, but don't worry, we're your friends, and we won't let them upset you," Hairstreak replied.

"ENOUGH CHIT CHAT!" yelled White Admiral. "This is not a party! You are not here to have fun! We are going to do circuit training now. Your bodies must be strong for your missions. Now start skipping!"

When they finished their gruelling exercise regime, they went back indoors to their dormitory to wash before attending their spy lessons in the classroom. Unfortunately, Grayling could not find his towel anywhere. As he looked round for it, he heard Adonis Blue, Clouded Yellow and Red Admiral all sniggering. Grayling realised that they had taken his towel and hidden it. Hairstreak, who had also heard them, offered his towel to Grayling, and in a loud voice, he said, "Here, Grayling, you can borrow mine," looking over at Team B as he said it; so they knew he was protecting his friend. Adonis Blue, Clouded Yellow and Red Admiral accepted defeat, gave up, and made their way to the classroom.

"Here are today's lessons; I hope you're paying attention, Agents!" White Admiral barked as he wrote on the whiteboard:

Lesson 1

How to become a master of disguise

Lesson 2

How to spy without being caught

Lesson 3

How to gather secret information unnoticed

Lesson 4

How to communicate covertly using your wings

Lesson 5

How to scare your enemy

Lesson 6

How to use your antennae for secret missions

After their intense lessons, the butterflies returned to their dormitory for a well-earned drink of delicious, sweet nectar. As they raised their glasses, Lady noticed that someone had sprinkled pollen into Grayling's drink. "Most butterflies don't eat pollen," she thought to herself. She grabbed the sugary liquid from Grayling and poured it over Adonis Blue's head, knowing full well that he was the offender. Adonis Blue was not pleased. "Grayling's friends keep ruining my plan!" he hissed at Clouded Yellow and Red Admiral.

Two exhausting days later, the butterflies finally finished their training. White Admiral stood in front of them for the last time. "I am pleased to tell you that you have all passed your training with top marks, and you are now ready to accept your missions. Remember, when you go out into the world, humans will see you as a symbol of hope, make us proud butterflies; our planet depends on your expertise in reacting to even the smallest of changes in the environment," he told them.

"At the beginning of your training," he continued, "I told you I would choose the best of the best for the most dangerous of the two missions awaiting you. I have been watching you all very closely, and the butterfly who achieved top marks in all his lessons, physical training and has shown the greatest strength of character is Grayling."

Hairstreak and Lady jumped with joy and gave Grayling a big hug, but Adonis Blue was not happy; he flew over to Clouded Yellow and Red Admiral. "I should have been chosen!" he sneered. "I won't let Grayling get away with this!"

"As you are the winner, Grayling," continued White Admiral, "you get to choose the two butterflies you want to work with on your mission." It didn't take Grayling long to make his choice.

"Agents Painted Lady and Green Hairstreak, Sir," he replied.

"Good," said White Admiral. "The three of you have an important assignment to carry out. We need you to find out where dragonflies live. Dragonflies are ecosystem indicators like butterflies, but they can do something we can't. Your mission is to find out what that is. Be careful, butterfly agents, as you will be in their territory. Remember your training, blend in, so they don't notice you. Now, go and good luck!"

Grayling, Lady and Hairstreak immediately left the spy school. They flew across the empty field, stopping briefly on a tree to plan their next move. Looking around to ensure no one could hear them, they started to talk. "We need to know where to find the dragonflies," whispered Grayling. "Lady, you flutter down to the grass and see if you can learn anything there, and Hairstreak, fly to the top of this tree and see what you can find out up there."

Lady swooped down and hovered for a while, then remembering her lesson on gathering secret information without being noticed, she pretended to drink nectar from a wildflower whilst listening intently to all the insects talking. Afterwards, she flew back to her fellow agents. "Hairstreak could not find any information. How about you, Lady?" Grayling asked her.

"Yes, I heard dragonflies like to live near water," replied Lady. "Word in the grass is that dragonflies eat any insects they catch, especially mosquitoes. They also eat butterflies, gnats, moths, bees, flies and even other dragonflies, so we must be careful not to get caught as they are very clever and catch their prey mid-air!"

"Good work, Lady. I can see a pond in the garden on the other side of the white picket fence. Let's go, but remember, if we need to communicate, we must either whisper or use our wings so no one can hear us. If we are in any danger, we must flap our wings twice as fast as normal," Grayling told them.

They flew over the white picket fence, past the vegetable patch, over a stone bird table, where a mischievous-looking cat was hiding and intently watching a couple of birds, and there, next to a little wooden shed, they found a small oval-shaped pond.

As they fluttered about in the air, they saw dragonflies hovering above the pond. One of the dragonflies began to fly towards them. "Quick! Camouflage!" ordered Grayling. Lady quickly perched on a flower and pretended to be a petal. Hairstreak immediately flew over to a bush and disguised himself as a leaf, and Grayling flew to a tree trunk and blended in with the bark. The dragonfly flew past, and Grayling used his wings to signal that the coast was clear. The three butterflies reunited and perched upon the little wooden shed to get a good view of the pond.

They watched the dragonflies busily darting about and skimming the surface of the water. "We need to get closer," said Hairstreak.

"If we get too close, they will catch and eat us," replied Lady.

"I have a plan," Grayling said. "We need to disguise ourselves as brightly coloured dragonflies. Hairstreak, wrap your bright wings round my body and Lady, I want you to pretend to be drinking nectar from one of the flowers by the pond. Wait there in case we are in danger and need your help."

Hairstreak wrapped his bright green wings round Grayling's body, and Grayling used his antennae to navigate them both towards the pond. "I'm going to put my antennae in front of my eyes and face like the dragonflies," Grayling told Hairstreak. "Hold on tight!"

In the meantime, Lady flew down to the pond, perched on top of an orange flower and pretended to drink nectar. Unnoticed, she peered through her transparent wings and watched Grayling and Hairstreak join the dazzling display of brightly coloured dragonflies.

"I'm really scared," whispered Hairstreak, trying not to tremble too much and ruin their disguise.

"Don't worry," Grayling reassured him. "We'll just hover with the dragonflies for a while, pretend to be one of them and find out what we can."

They proceeded with the plan, darting in and out of the dragonflies, whilst Grayling observed them intently. "What's happening?" asked Hairstreak, as he could not see anything.

"They are hunting and laying eggs in the water," replied Grayling. Then he gasped.

"What is it?" asked Hairstreak,

feeling frightened.

"I have just worked out what they can do that we can't!" Grayling exclaimed.

Unfortunately, before he could tell Hairstreak what that was, Grayling crashed straight into one of the dragonflies, losing his balance and dropping Hairstreak headfirst into the water. Grayling flapped his wings frantically to get the message to Lady that they were in trouble, just as the dragonfly he had bumped into used its long legs to capture him. Grayling tried to free himself, but the dragonfly's grip was too tight.

Lady flew into action. She swooped down and scooped Hairstreak out of the water, then slammed into the dragonfly, who had

Grayling. Luckily, the dragonfly lost its grip, and Grayling managed to escape, quickly flying away from the pond towards the safety and familiarity of the land, where he landed on top of a nearby flower. However, before he could catch his breath, he felt somebody shove him off the flower, and he plunged headfirst into the grass. Startled, he looked up and was astonished to see Adonis Blue standing over him. "Your friends are not here to help you now, Grayling," Adonis Blue snarled. "I will prove to White Admiral that I am the better spy! My colourful wings make me superior to you. Tell me what the dragonflies do, and I won't harm you!" he threatened.

"No!" cried Grayling. "I am the leader of this mission, and you will not stop me!"

Grayling and Adonis Blue started fighting, using their newfound combat training skills. They were equally as strong, neither willing to surrender. They rolled around in the grass, locked in battle. Adonis Blue managed to pin Grayling down, but just as he was going to win the fight, Grayling mustered enough energy to push Adonis Blue into the air. Adonis Blue bashed against the handle of an empty metal watering can that stood beside the pond and fell inside. Grayling flew to the handle and looked down at Adonis Blue. "You don't frighten me. I'm proud of who I am." Grayling told him as he looked up and saw Lady and Hairstreak watching over him. "When I am in trouble, my friends help me; that's what makes me strong, not the colour of my wings," he said, leaving Adonis Blue in the watering can as he flew over to join his teammates.

The three butterfly agents flew as fast as they could, over the vegetable patch and the white picket fence, through the empty field and straight back to the spy school. They found White Admiral and gave him the crucial information.

White Admiral looked at the agents with pride. "So, dragonflies are ecosystem indicators of water quality, and we are unsuitable for this because we live on the land. This information is of the utmost importance. Agents Grayling, Painted Lady and Green Hairstreak, I applaud you on a job well done! You have completed your mission with honour and courage," he told them in a soft, sincere voice. "You are the best spies we have ever had, and to reward you for your bravery, I give you permission to take time off to relax. You have earned it, Agents.

Congratulations!"

The three exhausted butterflies flew away, looking forward to their rest. "Let's go home," said Grayling. "My family live near the coast; if you like, you can come back with me?" he suggested. However, before Lady and Hairstreak could answer, the butterflies were distracted by a small piece of folded paper embedded in a nearby hedgerow. They flew over and unfolded it. There was a mysterious message inside:

TO GRAYLING, LADY AND HAIRSTREAK

YOUR PRESENCE HAS BEEN REQUESTED

GO TO THE VEGETABLE PATCH AT SUNRISE

3. THE BIRDS

Fangs did not like birds in his garden, and he had been trying to catch Robin and Starling for months. Each time they somehow managed to get away, making him increasingly frustrated. "Not this time!" he thought as he cunningly hid behind the stone bird table and waited for them to appear.

Fangs was a long-haired tabby cat; his stripy, brown and cream fur had a yellow tinge, and his pointy ears, which helped him catch even the smallest of prey, were yellow with tufts of cream hair inside them. His sinister-looking, yellow eyes had a black outline, making him look like a highwayman; he wanted to look mean, and he did.

Fangs led a double life. In the family home, he was a pampered lap cat. He purred and rubbed round his owners' legs, looking up at them with hypnotic eyes, bewitching them into giving him a bowl of delicious cream or a soft blanket by the fire. However, outside in the garden, he was a ruthless hunter. When he was on the prowl, the mice scampered, the birds flew away, and the frogs jumped back into the pond. Even the rabbits would scurry down their burrows for protection. He was a predator who did not always kill his prey for food; he did it for sport.

But ... Fangs had a secret ... a secret that only he knew. A secret that he would take to the grave.

Suddenly, his thoughts were interrupted when he saw Starling fly down into the garden.

"Robin! Where are you?" Starling shouted, looking round for her friend. Perched upon the handle of a metal watering can that stood by a small oval-shaped pond, Starling had a good view of the garden from the ivy-covered house, all the way to the white picket fence next to the vegetable patch. She heard a faint splashing sound as a frog jumped into the pond and hid under a lily pad. "Oh no! Fangs must be nearby," she thought, feeling slightly uneasy. "HURRY UP, ROBIN! We must solve the mystery of the stolen jewellery as soon as possible!" she yelled impatiently.

Slowly, an orange-red-faced head poked out of a dark green

Wellington boot hidden behind a dustbin next to the kitchen door at the back of the house.

"Stop shouting, Starling! Why do you always have to be so noisy? I'm coming!" Robin snapped. First, looking round to ensure he was safe, he hopped out of his Wellington boot home and joined his friend on the top of the watering can.

Robin did not like being out in the open for too long; he preferred to be hidden away, unlike Starling, who loved open spaces. He adored his garden and passionately guarded the little area he called home. Robin enjoyed silence so he could think about things, like where he would find his next meal of yummy worms or how he could keep his Wellington boot house neat and tidy.

He was quiet, except for the odd song he liked to sing, and enjoyed hopping on things like the wheelbarrow, garden tools and flowerpots. Sometimes, he would keep the family who lived in the house company whilst they did their gardening. It was a peaceful life, and that's how he liked it.

Starling was the opposite of Robin. She was lively and chatty and nested in a small colony that was always noisy, especially at feeding times. She and her flock took great pleasure in entertaining everyone with their spectacular acrobatic displays in the sky. Starling loved having an audience and being the star of the show. "After all, you can't spell my name without 'STAR' in it," she would tell anyone who was listening. After her lively evenings out dancing, swooping and twisting, she and her family would contentedly huddle up together to keep safe and warm for the night. Starling's wings looked black from a distance, but close-up, they were purple and green with little white spots.

Although Robin and Starling had completely opposite personalities and came from different backgrounds, they were the best of friends.

"Look what I found!" Starling gushed with excitement. "A book on how to be a detective. It will help us find out who stole the jewellery from the family who live in the house." Starling lifted the book she had kept hidden behind the watering can and opened it with her beak.

"The first thing we need to do is wear a detective hat and carry a magnifying glass," she said as she handed the crucial tools to Robin. Robin put on the hat; it went well with his orange-red breast and brown wings. Starling's eyes appeared enormous as she looked through the magnifying glass. "We look like Sherlock Holmes," Robin laughed.

"The book says we need to write down who our suspects are," Starling noted.

"I'll do the writing," offered Robin. "I'm good at writing; you're better at talking," he giggled. Starling gave Robin a notebook and a pencil. "OK. Write this down," she told him. "A murder of crows, a conspiracy of ravens and a mischief of magpies. See? Murder, conspiracy and mischief!

These birds sound very suspicious; I think we should investigate them all. One of these groups MUST be the jewel thieves," Starling deduced.

"Good idea!" agreed Robin. "Let's search for their nests, one by one, and find out who stole the jewellery!"

As they chatted, Fangs, who had been watching them intently, licked his lips as he pictured them on his dinner plate. He slowly crouched down, his bottom started to wiggle, his whiskers began to twitch, and his mischievous, yellow eyes squinted as he got ready to pounce.

"FLY!" screamed Starling. She and Robin flew into the air as Fangs narrowly missed them, crashing into the metal watering can and falling to the floor in bewilderment. He was not happy. "Next time, I will catch you!" he shouted angrily at the birds as they flew away.

"Phew, that was a lucky escape," Robin said. "Come on, let's go and find the crows' nest first and see if the jewellery is there.

They swooped over to an old oak tree where the crows had been building their twig nest all through the spring and hid behind a branch full of leaves. "The crows aren't here; let's investigate," Robin whispered. However, before they got near the nest, Starling was distracted by something on the ground. "Look! Down there!" she cried, pointing to some marks in the dry soil at the base of the tree.

They flew down to have a closer inspection. Starling used her magnifying glass to look at the marks more clearly. "They look like pawprints," she concluded. "Draw them in the notebook, Robin; I think they are our first clue. I wonder to whom they belong. A fox? A hedgehog? A badger?" she asked. "Let's follow them and see where they lead to."

Robin and Starling followed the animal tracks, which took them all the way to a thorny bush at the bottom of the garden and then all the way back up to the old oak tree again, at which point they noticed rough, jagged scratch marks etched into the bark at its base. "Look! I don't know who made those marks, but I think they might be another clue," Starling said.

"I deduce that it must have been

an animal," answered Robin, feeling like a real detective.

"Make a tracing of the scratch marks in the notebook, Robin, and we can look at it later," Starling suggested. Robin placed the paper from the notebook on top of the markings and rubbed the pencil over them.

When he had finished, they excitedly flew back up to the crows' nest, expecting to find the jewellery. However, they were disappointed that their only discovery was a bewildered-looking caterpillar who had made a wrong turn. "The crows did not steal the jewellery," Starling sighed. "You can cross them off our list of suspects. Come on, let's find the ravens."

On their way to find the ravens,

they decided to stop at the pond for a drink. The pond was next to a little wooden shed where the family kept all their gardening equipment. They hopped onto the edge and drank the cool, clear water. Suddenly, they heard a loud "MEOW" followed by a BANG! They looked round and saw Fangs with his head stuck in a bucket and his bottom in the air. Robin and Starling laughed. "You missed us again, Fangs!" they shouted as they flew off.

"Where do ravens live?" Robin asked Starling.

"I think they like to nest in tall trees," Starling answered. "Look! I can see their nest in the beech tree over there. Let's hide until the coast is clear," she suggested pointing to a rose bush at the foot of the tree. They quietly sneaked up behind the bush and, to their surprise, stumbled upon a pile of bones. "What kind of bones are they?" Starling asked, astonished at their discovery.

"I don't know," answered Robin. "I'll sketch them in the notebook just in case they are a clue." He took out the notebook and drew a sketch of the bones and wrote, 'Clue Number 3' with a question mark next to it.

When the coast was finally clear, they flew up into the beech tree and peeked inside the nest, but, to their dismay, they did not find any jewellery, just a pile of moss and some twigs. "Well, it's not the ravens either. You can cross them off our list too, Robin," Starling said, feeling disheartened.

They flew over and perched on the white picket fence at the end of the garden to discuss their findings but immediately flew off when they felt a sudden shudder. They looked down and saw Fangs, his body; flat as a pancake, sliding down one of the panels. He had misjudged the height of the fence as he pounced at the birds and smashed against it. He was furious. "You'll have to do better than that, Fangs!" Robin and Starling giggled as they flew away.

The two friends flew to the stone bird table for a little snack of tasty bird seed. As they ate, they discussed their case. "The magpies must be the culprits. I bet we find the stolen jewellery in their nest," said Starling.

"Magpies like to build their nests in thorny bushes. There's one at the end of the garden, next to the vegetable patch and the beehive; let's take a look," Robin suggested, and off they went.

"That's strange; the beehive is surrounded by menacing-looking wasps," remarked Starling as they flew past the vegetable patch. Nevertheless, they were soon distracted when they saw a large, dome-shaped nest made from twigs and sticks in the middle of the thorny bush. There was a small opening to the side of it, so they peered inside, and there, nestled in the mud interior, they found the sparkling gems. "The stolen jewellery!" cried Starling. "It was the magpies, after all!"

When the magpies returned to their nest, Robin and Starling shouted, "JEWEL THIEVES! We caught you!"

The magpies looked very confused. They glanced at the sparkling jewellery and then up at Robin and Starling and pleaded their innocence. "It wasn't us, detectives. We promise! Everyone thinks we like shiny objects, but we don't; they scare us. Someone has put them in our nest to blame us for the crime. We did not steal the jewellery."

Robin and Starling knew that the magpies were telling the truth. "We believe you, magpies," they said. Feeling baffled, they flew to the roof of the little wooden shed and opened the notebook to inspect the clues, hoping to find the answer.

Clue number 1 - the pawprints

They checked the drawing against the pawprints in their detective book. The pawprints did not belong to a fox, a hedgehog or a badger; they belonged to a cat!

Clue number 2 - the scratch marks on the tree

They looked at the tracing of the scratch marks in the notebook. "They could have been made by a rabbit, a vole or a squirrel; how will we find out?" Robin questioned.

"What's that?" asked Starling, pointing to something stuck on the tracing.

"It's a cat's claw!" answered Robin. "It must have fallen off the bark when I was tracing and somehow wedged into the notebook. The marks must belong to a cat; they scratch trees to mark their territory, remove old claws and keep their new ones clean and sharp."

Clue number 3? - the bones

Robin looked at the sketch of the bones, but he could not work out what they were. He turned the notebook upside down to see it from a different perspective and instantly recognised them. "They are fish bones!" he exclaimed.

"There aren't any fish in the pond," responded Starling. "So, how did the fish bones get into the garden?"

Robin thought for a moment. "I did hear a "meow" coming from the dustbin outside the kitchen door yesterday after the family had cooked fish for their dinner. So, I think a cat must have taken the bones from the dustbin and left them in the garden," he answered.

All the clues pointed to one

animal. A CAT! Suddenly, they heard a sound behind them; they turned round and saw Fangs about to pounce.

"FANGS! YOU ARE THE JEWEL THIEF!" they exclaimed, pointing at him.

"Yes," replied Fangs. "I don't like birds in my garden; I wanted the magpies to be accused of the crime so my human family would chase them away, but you two meddling sleuths have ruined my plan! Now I will finally catch you and eat you for my dinner!"

Fangs took one last leap at the birds but tripped and fell off the shed roof. The birds heard a loud SPLASH! They looked down and saw a very angry Fangs sitting in the shallow end of the pond, splashing and spitting out lily pads from his mouth. The birds laughed so much that Robin's detective hat fell off his head and landed on one of Fangs' ears.

"We did it!" cried Robin. "We solved the mystery of the stolen jewellery; we are real detectives. Let's return the jewellery to its rightful owners."

The two birds flew through an open window of the house, into the kitchen, up the stairs, entered the big bedroom and placed the stolen jewellery on the dressing table. Before they left, Robin got out the notebook and pencil and wrote 'Clue Number 4' and drew a little drawing of a cat. He then balanced the notebook against the jewellery so the family could see what Fangs had done.

They flew back downstairs, and just as they were about to make their way out of the kitchen window, Robin stopped suddenly and perched on top of the fridge. "Wait!" he told Starling, who stopped and joined him. "Look over there at Fangs' food bowl; it has the name 'Fluffy' on it ... and look at Fangs' bed and his water bowl; they also have the name 'Fluffy' on them! I think Fangs has a secret he has been hiding from us," he said.

Robin and Starling looked at each other and laughed so hard that they fell off the fridge and rolled onto the floor. When they eventually composed themselves, they flew back out into the garden.

They settled on top of the metal watering can as they had done at the beginning of the day, but this time, they noticed something inside it. Robin hopped in to investigate and found that it was a small piece of folded paper. He picked it up with his beak, and he and Starling unfolded it. There was a mysterious message inside:

TO ROBIN AND STARLING

YOUR PRESENCE HAS BEEN REQUESTED

GO TO THE VEGETABLE PATCH AT SUNRISE

4. SUNRISE

The following morning, the rising sun gradually lit up the vegetable patch, and there, all together for the first time, were Betty, Grayling, Lady, Hairstreak, Robin and Starling. They looked at each other curiously. "What are we doing here?" asked Betty breaking the silence.

At that moment, a grey heron wearing a black hooded cloak swooped down and perched on top of the white picket fence. He towered over the pollinators enveloping them in the shadow of his outstretched wings, hiding them under a cloak of darkness. He then carefully removed the hood from his head, revealing his long neck, long beak, white face and distinctive black stripe.

The pollinators looked up at the

giant bird in awe and fear, frozen to the spot, unable to move their legs or speak. The .heron looked down and addressed his captive audience, answering Betty's question.

"Pay attention, pollinators; I cannot stay long. You are here because you have been chosen to undertake a top secret mission. I cannot tell you what your assignment will be, but you will find out soon enough, so be ready to leave at a moment's notice. There is one more thing you need to know. You are only half the team. You must find the rest of your teammates before you accept the mission. Good luck!"

The magnificent bird put his hood back on and began to fly away.

"Wait!" cried Betty, now able to speak again. "Who are our other teammates?" she asked.

The heron turned round and said, "All I can tell you is that they are the same as you but different."

And with that, he flew away as

mysteriously as he had arrived.

The pollinators shook their heads in disbelief, stunned and baffled by what had just happened.

"Who are the others, and where do we find them?"

"And how can they be the same as us but different?"

"What will our mission be, and when will we be told about it?"

The pollinators did not have the answers to their questions, but they did know that they were now part of something of the utmost importance, and it would change their lives forever. They agreed the best way forward was to carry on as normal until such time as something brought them together again.

5. THE BEETLES, BATS AND MOTHS

Later that night ...

"LET'S GO ON STRIKE!" Cole, the Cockchafer beetle, shouted as loudly as he could. The moonlight bounced off his reddish-brown wing case and cast a rusty glow over the faces of the night-time insects gazing up at him. "It's not fair!" he insisted. "Why do the daytime pollinators get all the attention whilst the night-time pollinators get none? Beetles, like me, are great at picking up sticky pollen grains on our bodies as we munch on flowers and leaves. I know I sometimes get confused and mistake chimney stacks for treetops, but I always get to the trees in the end!" he confessed, inciting the night-time insects to break into rapturous applause.

Cole cared deeply about night-time pollinators, especially beetles, not because he felt he was both those things but because he believed beetles were the first pollinators on earth. "Beetles were pollinating plants since before the time of the dinosaurs," he would boast.

Nevertheless, speaking out on behalf of pollinators was just one side of Cole's personality; unfortunately, the other side was his clumsiness. It was difficult for him to fly in a straight line, and he kept bumping into things, especially windowpanes and humans. Cole was always getting into scrapes and relied on his friends to keep him out of trouble.

As the insects roared with excitement, Cole desperately looked round the garden for his best friends: Bram and Beth, the Pipistrelle bats and Paige, Parker and Penelope, the Pine Hawk-moths, but they were nowhere in sight. "They must be here somewhere," he thought, hoping to see them appear at any moment.

Unfortunately, Bram and Beth were preoccupied. They were hunting near the old oak tree, in close pursuit of two fugitive mosquitoes. "You can't get away from us, mosquitoes!" Beth called out. "Bram and I are in a hurry to help our best friend, so if you think you can hide from us, you are mistaken!"

A little caterpillar snuggled up in the crows' nest, popped its head up and watched the bats fly past.

Beth took a moment to look at the Wanted Poster the pigeons had given her. It read:

WANTED

DEAD, ALIVE OR EATEN

FOR FEEDING ON THE BLOOD OF A PIGEON

Two outlaw mosquitoes
Thin, long bodies, three pairs of long legs and hairy antennae

Satisfied that she and Bram were chasing the right mosquitoes, the two bats swiftly dived in and out of the branches. They briefly looked down at a rowdy insect crowd that had gathered and saw Cole standing in front of them, his fanned, orange antennae swaying from side to side.

"Oh no! I think Cole is about to topple over!" Bram told Beth. "Let's hurry and catch the mosquitoes before he gets into trouble again."

The mosquitoes cleverly used the distraction of the noisy insects to dart from the old oak tree to the small oval -shaped pond in order to escape the hunters and lay their eggs in the water. Unfortunately, they did not realise that Bram and Beth would use their ultrasonic sound waves to find them. When the echo bounced back, the bats swooped in and ate the mosquitoes mid-air. "Good job!" said Beth as she and Bram high-fived each other. "The pigeons will be pleased when we tell them we've eaten the mosquitoes. Now, we must go down and help Cole before he has an accident!" Their small, brown bodies and black wings carried them down to their friend.

Meanwhile, Paige, Parker and Penelope, Cole's other best friends, were in a difficult situation. They had been hypnotised and trapped by the Honeysuckle plant, which had used its seductive, sweet perfume and delicious nectar to capture them.

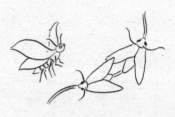

The Honeysuckle, which adorned the white picket fence at the end of the garden, was full of beautiful flowers in romantic shades of pink and cream that shimmered in the moonlight. When it saw the Pine Hawk-moths approaching, it deviously lured them in with a magnetic, musky aroma they could not resist. The scheming plant had no intention of ever letting them go.

"We must get away; Cole needs

us! You know what will happen if we don't help him; he will plummet into the pond!" Paige cried as she tried in vain to stop drinking the fruity nectar.

"Just a tiny bit more; it's so tasty," pleaded Penelope.

"Yes, let's stay just a little longer," agreed Parker enjoying the sugary liquid.

The three moths slowly succumbed to the Honeysuckle's spellbinding power, and their beetle friend faded from their minds.

Suddenly, a loud rapture of applause jolted the moths back to reality. "Penelope! Parker! We must resist the Honeysuckle's charms!" Paige shouted. The Honeysuckle retaliated by releasing a sweeter scent into the night air, but it was too late, the spell had broken, and the moths were set free. They managed to escape and fly away. "Whatever you do, DO NOT look back at the plant and DO NOT smell its perfume!" Paige urged.

Cole looked round again, and to his relief, he saw Bram and Beth swooping down from the old oak tree and then recognised the outline of Paige, Parker and Penelope's arrow-shaped, grey-brown wings coming from the direction of the white picket fence. They got there in time to catch Cole just as he was about to fall off the handle of the metal watering can he was standing on.

"...Take the daytime garden birds, for example," Cole continued with his speech. "They don't even know they are pollinating! They accidentally carry pollen on their feathers and feet and move it round the garden. They are not true pollinators like the Hummingbirds, Honeyeaters and Sunbirds who live abroad. Yet, everyone wants birds in their gardens, and they feed them! Nobody ever feeds or welcomes us beetles into their gardens," Cole protested.

"We are angry too!" the moths joined in. "Everybody calls us ugly butterflies! We are NOT ugly! And we pollinate just as well as they do, if not better! We drink nectar and carry pollen on our tongues. Our bodies may be furry, but that's a good thing because pollen sticks to us," they explained.

The bats also wanted to have a say on the matter. "We, Pipistrelle bats, are not pollinators," they interrupted, "but our bat family abroad are! They are vital night-time pollinators; we wouldn't have bananas without them! They pollinate the night blooming banana plant flowers," Bram and Beth said with pride.

"I SAY WE GO ON STRIKE! WHO'S WITH ME?" Cole yelled. The crowd, who were already at fever pitch, erupted into cheers.

"I'm not sure it's a good idea to go on strike, Cole," the bats disagreed. "Night-time pollinators' jobs are too important to stop just like that, but we do agree that we need to do something to show the daytime pollinators that they are not better than us!"

Paige, Parker and Penelope agreed with Bram and Beth. "Rather than go on strike, why don't we sabotage their environment instead!" There was another roar from the insect crowd.

"We are agreed! I will make sure that the daytime pollinators do not get all the attention," Cole promised and promptly called the gathering to an end.

As the insects departed and went their separate ways, Cole flew down from the top of the watering can under the watchful eyes of his friends. "We need a plan," he told them. "How do nocturnal pollinators sabotage the daytime pollinators' environment? We are asleep when they are awake!" he asked.

"We need someone awake in the daytime and the night-time to help us. Someone who doesn't like the daytime pollinators either," the bats agreed. They all tried to figure out who that someone could be.

Suddenly, they heard a loud CRASH, followed by a THUD. The pollinators turned round and saw Fangs sitting on his bottom in a daze, a dustbin lid balancing on his head and fishbones dangling from his ears. He had unsuccessfully tried to climb into the dustbin at the back of the ivy-covered house to get hold of the fishbones but slipped, banged his head and managed to bring the dustbin down with him.

Cole, Bram, Beth, Paige, Parker and Penelope looked at each other and laughed. "I think we have found our saboteur," said the moths. The night-time pollinators flew over and perched on the fallen dustbin. They told Fangs their plan and asked if he would help them.

Fangs, who was still angry with Robin and Starling for getting him into trouble with his human family and, even worse, for revealing to everyone that his real name was Fluffy, was eager for a chance to get his revenge on them. "I'm in!" he said with a wicked smile. "I wasn't allowed to sleep on my comfy bed for a week because of those pesky birds! What's more, now that everyone knows my real name, I need to do something to get my mean reputation back," he told them.

Cole thought for a moment. "Bees are drawn towards bright coloured flowers, aren't they? Could you try to cover the flowers with something, Fangs, so they can't see them?" he asked.

"And... butterflies are attracted to the fragrant perfume of the flowers. Would you be able to mask the smell somehow, Fangs?" asked Paige.

"Also, is there any chance you could frighten the birds away from the garden, so they can't hop round the bushes and trees and accidentally pollinate them?" asked Beth.

Fangs took one of the fishbones dangling from his ear, placed it in his mouth and licked it slowly whilst he thought. "Hmm, yes, I can do all those things," he purred.

Later that morning ...

Moments before the sun pierced through the darkness; Fangs went into a frenzy of activity; he knew he didn't have much time before the daytime pollinators woke up. His first job was to cover the flowers so the bees could not see their bright colours. Racing against time, he sprinted from the back of the ivy-covered house to the vegetable patch at the end of the garden, deciding that the best way to hide the bright colours was to cover all the flowers in mud. One by one, he dug and scooped up the soil in the flower beds and splattered the flower petals with it, using his hind legs. He took extra special care to cover the beautiful flowers of a Honeysuckle plant wrapped round the white picket fence.

Then, he darted into the house through the cat flap, leapt up the stairs and found the dirty laundry basket, which was brimming with dirty socks. "Humans have very smelly feet!" he thought as he put a peg on his nose to hide the unpleasant odour. He reluctantly picked up the smelly socks with his mouth, dashed back downstairs and jumped out through the cat flap as quickly as he could. He placed the stinky items round the flowers. "Yuck!" he thought.

After that, he sent out a distress signal to all his cat neighbours. Immediately, cats of varying colours and sizes from all over the neighbourhood jumped over the fences that enclosed the garden and joined him. Fangs asked them to hide behind the bushes, as far up in the trees as they could manage, on the roof of the little wooden shed, next to the beehive, and, if they saw any birds, their instructions were to frighten and chase them away. "Except for Robin and Starling," he said menacingly. "They are mine!"

Fangs then went back to the house, curled up on his little cat bed and collapsed with exhaustion.

The sun rose steadfastly in the east, prompting the daylight wildlife to wake up from their night-time slumber and start their busy working days. Betty, now a pollinator, flew out of the beehive with her fellow pollinating worker bees to collect food and water for the colony. Cheerfully buzzing to herself as she dreamed of soon wearing the prestigious Stingerteers uniform, she made her way to the flower beds.

However, she soon realised something was amiss. "That's

strange," she said to her fellow pollinating worker bees. "I can't see any flowers." The bees flew the length and breadth of the garden, but they could not find them anywhere. "Where have all the flowers gone, and what will we tell the Queen?" asked one of the bees. "She will banish us from the hive if we don't come back with pollen and nectar."

Betty was quiet. "Something is wrong," she thought to herself.

At the same time, Grayling, Lady and Hairstreak idly fluttered about in the garden, enjoying their well-earned rest and the morning sunshine. "Let's have a lovely drink of sweet nectar," suggested Lady.

"Yes," replied Hairstreak. However, they had to abandon that idea because they could not pick up the sweet, delicate scent of the plants. "I can't smell any flowers," said Hairstreak, feeling confused. "All I can detect is a waft of smelly feet in the air!"

Grayling pondered for a moment. "Something is wrong," he told them.

The sun, now in its midday position, shone down on Robin as he flew over to the metal watering can from his Wellington boot home to meet his best friend, Starling. "The garden is oddly quiet today," he said. "I can't hear any birds singing, can you?" Robin asked her.

"No, and I haven't seen any birds either; I think you and I are the only ones here," she replied, looking round the garden. "Robin! Don't look now, but over there, I can see a black tail behind the old oak tree and a ginger tail behind the flowerpot! I can also see two stripey grey ears poking out from the roof of the little wooden shed and three cats up in the branches of the beech tree. "Oh no! It's a trap! FLY!" Starling screamed.

At that moment, Fangs flew out from behind the stone bird table, narrowly missing the two birds and landing on top of a prickly bush. "OUCH!" he yelped in pain as he watched the birds escape him yet again.

Robin and Starling flew to the top of the tallest tree where the cats couldn't reach them and whistled a signal to Betty, Grayling, Lady and Hairstreak. Before long, they were all together again. "Something is wrong!" Robin announced.

"Yes," agreed Betty. "The other bees and I can't find the flowers."

"We can't smell them," Grayling added, speaking on behalf of the butterflies.

"Starling and I think that Fangs has something to do with this," said Robin. "He is always trying to find ways to catch us, but what is puzzling is why he is sabotaging our environment?"

"All the clues point to someone who wants to stop the daytime pollinators from doing their jobs," Starling said, "but who would want to do that?"

"I think we should stay awake tonight and follow Fangs. I'm sure he will lead us to the culprit," Hairstreak suggested.

"Good idea!" agreed Betty. "Let's all meet up at the vegetable patch at sunset and follow him." The others concurred and then flew away.

Later that evening ...

As the sun disappeared below the horizon, the daytime pollinators met up and hid amongst the large leaves of a rhubarb plant growing in the vegetable patch. "I don't like the dark," confessed Lady.

"Me neither," replied Robin.

"What's that scary noise?" asked Betty.

"I think it's an owl," answered Starling.

"What's that ball in the sky?" asked Grayling.

"I'm not sure, but it could be the moon?" replied Hairstreak.

The pollinators felt out of place in the darkness, missing the safety and familiarity of daylight. Nevertheless, they didn't have to wait long before Fangs strolled past. He was on the prowl, looking for an innocent little mouse to torment. "Shh, everyone. Let's follow him," whispered Grayling. The daytime pollinators quietly flew behind Fangs, hiding behind trees and bushes as they went. "Wait," said Betty. "I think he's stopping. Look! I can see some bats swooping down."

"Yes, and three moths," added Lady.

"There's a beetle, too," Starling noticed. They stopped by a tree and listened to what Fangs and the night-time pollinators were saying.

"Did you sabotage the daytime pollinators' environment?" Cole asked Fangs.

"Yes," replied Fangs, "but I didn't manage to catch those two infuriating birds!" he hissed.

"What else can we do to stop them pollinating?" asked Parker. However, before anyone was able to answer his question, the daytime pollinators flew out from behind the tree and caught the night-time pollinators by surprise. The shock of seeing them caused Cole to bump into the bats and moths, and they all fell to the ground.

"Why are you trying to sabotage our environment?" the daytime pollinators demanded. Once the night-time pollinators had got back up onto their legs, Cole replied on their behalf. "We are fed up with you trying to take all the glory! We are just as important as you!" he cried.

"I know how important beetles are," Betty replied softly. "I helped save Princess Mina because she helps the oil beetles survive," she told Cole.

"We need you, moths," the butterflies joined in. "We can only pollinate the daytime flowers; we rely on you to drink the nectar of the night blooming flowers; their beautiful fragrance is strongest when the sun goes down to attract you, not us."

"Starling and I try to eat as many insects as we can to clear the way for the bees," Robin added, "but you are the best insect-hunters around, bats; we can't eat as many as you do; you eat thousands a night!" he told them enviously.

The night-time pollinators suddenly felt ashamed that they had caused so many problems for the daytime pollinators; they had not realised how appreciated they were. "We're sorry," they humbly apologised. Fangs, who was now bored with the conversation, had become much more interested in following an unsuspecting little vole he had spied. The pollinators laughed as they watched the vole getting the better of him by escaping into an underground burrow it had dug earlier, leaving Fangs with his head stuck in the hole and his bottom waving in the air!

The daytime pollinators looked at each other, thinking the same thing; they had inadvertently done what the mysterious grey heron in the black hooded cloak had told them to do. They had found the other half of their team. Grayling put their thoughts into words. "We have been chosen to undertake a top secret mission; would you like to join us?" he proposed to the night-time pollinators.

Cole, Bram, Beth, Paige, Parker and Penelope were astonished. Feeling loved and valued, they cried, "YES!" at the top of their voices.

"Wonderful!" Betty exclaimed. "We will make a great team. Together, we are not just pollinators; we are The Powerful Pollinators!"

At that moment, they heard something overhead. The Powerful Pollinators looked up and noticed a tiny box attached to a little parachute slowly making its way down.

"What is it?" asked Penelope.

Robin and Starling helped Paige and Parker catch the box, and they opened it. Inside was a piece of paper, but it was blank. "There must be secret writing on it," Lady told them, remembering one of her lessons at spy school.

"Yes, let's tilt it towards the moon and see if the writing appears," agreed Bram and Beth. When the moonlight lit the piece of paper up, it revealed a message:

TOP SECRET

ATTENTION POWERFUL POLLINATORS

YOU HAVE BEEN CHOSEN TO UNDERTAKE A TOP SECRET MISSION

THE WILFUL WILDFLOWER MUSES ARE IN DANGER. THEY NEED YOUR HELP IMMEDIATELY

IF YOU CHOOSE TO ACCEPT THIS MISSION YOU MUST LEAVE NOW

THIS MESSAGE WILL SELF-COMBUST IN 30 SECONDS

It took a while for The Powerful Pollinators to digest what they had just read, but the excitement of the message soon swept over them. "WE ACCEPT! LET'S GO AND RESCUE THE WILFUL WILDFLOWER MUSES!" they cried in unison. As they flew into the night air, Grayling and Hairstreak grabbed Cole just as he was about to fly into the piece of paper as it went up in smoke.

From
The Wilful Wildflowers
and The Woeful Witch

"I am going to turn you all into
Muses so that you can inspire
beauty and art wherever you go."

.... Circe waved her wand for the
last time and in a swirl of scarlet,
gold, rose and white fairy dust,
The Wilful Wildflowers were
transformed into The Wilful
Wildflower Muses.